TRANSFER TROUBLE

KEITH BRUMPTON

USBORNE

Go to www.keithbrumpton.co.uk
for more on Terry and the team.

First published in 2011 by Usborne Publishing Ltd., Usborne House,
83-85 Saffron Hill, London EC1N 8RT, England.
www.usborne.com

A CIP catalogue record for this book is available from the British Library.

JFMAMJ ASOND/17 ISBN 9781409538202 00040/5
Printed in India.

DINO FC

Dear Dino-soccer fan,
A warm welcome to today's visitors, whoever they are (Steggy Stegoceras borrowed my fixture list and he hasn't returned it yet). The squad's been training hard as we have some crunch games coming up and we don't want to get crunched.

  I hope today's match provides the usual thrills and spills you come to see. We'll certainly be working hard to win the three points and continue our climb up the table!

  All the best
  TERRY TRICERATOPS

DINO FC LINE-UP

CYRIL STEGOSAURUS
FULLBACK

STEGGY STEGOCERAS
DEFENDER

PTERADONNA
GOALKEEPER

MARCUS DIPLODOCUS
DEFENDER

TERRY TRICERATOPS
MANAGER / FULLBACK

ARCHIE OPTERYX
LEFT WINGER

ALBERT ALLOSAURUS
CENTRE MIDFIELD

CELIA COELOPHYSIS
FORWARD

GWEN CORYTHOSAURUS
CENTRE MIDFIELD

JOSÉ HETERODONTOSAURUS
FORWARD

ERIC ALLOSAURUS
RIGHT MIDFIELD

TODAY'S SUB:

OLLIE OVIRAPTOR
FORWARD

CHAPTER 1

Dino FC player-manager, Terry Triceratops, had just been in a meeting with club chairman Danny Deinonychus. They'd been discussing the transfer budget.

THESE ARE DIFFICULT TIMES FOR BILLIONAIRES LIKE MYSELF.

Possible transfer targets

"How much have you got?" asked Terry's loyal vice captain, Cyril Stegosaurus, who had been waiting for him in the corridor outside Danny's office.

"Well it's got a nought in it," answered Terry, a little gloomily.

AND WHAT OTHER NUMBERS?

NONE. JUST A NOUGHT!

Cyril now knew why his boss was looking so glum. It seemed the Dino FC transfer kitty was emptier than ever.

Cyril suddenly turned a very pale shade of green. He had played badly in the team's last match.

Terry put a consoling hoof around Cyril's shoulders.

> DON'T WORRY, CYRIL. I'VE GOT NO INTENTION OF TRANSFERRING YOU. THERE CAN'T BE ANY BETTER FULLBACKS IN THE DINO PREMIERSHIP.

Cyril looked hugely relieved.

Terry's face assumed a thoughtful expression.

> NO, OF ALL THE PLAYERS IN MY SQUAD, THERE'S ONLY ONE I WOULD THINK ABOUT PUTTING ON THE TRANSFER LIST...

The Dino FC treatment room wasn't anything fancy (Dino being a small and cash-strapped team). In fact it consisted of nothing more than a small cave with a hot spring in the middle and a long stone slab.

Centre forward José Heterodontosaurus was supposed to be there doing some exercises for a tail strain he claimed to have suffered in a recent match.

José always seemed to have a lot of injuries and was rarely on the pitch for the full ninety minutes. Some fans – and even teammates – suspected that he wasn't really injured at all, but just didn't like playing when the going got tough.

And right now, José didn't seem too

badly injured – in fact he was on the phone to his agent, Eddie "Fastbuck" Euparkeria. José spoke to his agent three or four times a day, usually to try and get a wage increase, or a transfer to a bigger team, or both.

EDDIE? THIS IS JOSÉ. NO THE TAIL IS NOT SO GOOD...VERY SORE...MAYBE I MISS THE NEXT GAME...

José lay somewhat theatrically back on the stone treatment slab and wearily closed his eyes.

"They play so very much in this Dino Premiership. *Every* week. And the guys I play with, always I stand in the perfect place to score, but they make mistake and I do not get the ball. *Por favor*...I would like to play in some other league...for a good team like Real Heterodontosaurus...who have the good players, like me..."

There was a pause on the line before Eddie answered.

JOSÉ, I'M MAKING CALLS. TRUST ME... I'M TRYING TO GET YOU THE BIG MOVE. BUT IT DOESN'T HELP WHEN YOU ARE ALWAYS INJURED.

José suddenly looked the liveliest he had been all day. He leaped angrily from the treatment slab.

And with that, José's call to his agent ended. He lay back on the slab and began stretching out his tail very gingerly.

PROGRESS
REPORT
(SECRET)
INFO

Terry was working in his office. He looked
again at the progress reports he had written
for each player at the club.

He was checking for strengths and
weaknesses, making sure that the player he
had decided to transfer really was the one
to get rid of. Releasing players was one of
the few things Terry hated about his job, but

he knew he would need to make his decision quickly because the Dino Premiership transfer deadline was only forty-eight hours away. And after that, no more players could be bought or sold until the season ended.

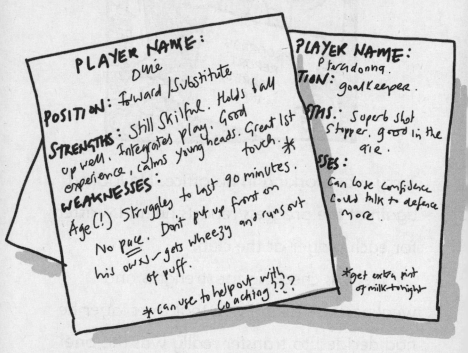

PLAYER NAME: Dixie

POSITION: Forward /Substitute

STRENGTHS: Still Skilful. Holds ball up well. Integrates play. Good experience, calms young heads. Great 1st touch. *

WEAKNESSES: Age (!) Struggles to last 90 minutes. No pace. Don't put up front on his own ~ gets wheezy and runs out of puff.

* can use to help out with coaching ???

PLAYER NAME: Pterodonna.

POSITION: goalkeeper.

STRENGTHS: Superb shot stopper. good in the air.

WEAKNESSES: Can lose confidence Could talk to defence more.

*get extra pint of milk tonight

Terry gathered up his papers and gave a yawn. It had been another hard day and he was exhausted. But deep down he knew the choice he had made was the right one. He hoped everyone else would agree when he made his announcement the next day...

PLAYER NAME: CElia

POSITION: forward

STRENGTHS: Scores goals. great pace. good amitude.

WEAKNESSES: Doesn't look up when crossing the ball! Too keen on talking to the press. Shooting could be better.
* would like to try in midfield some time.

NAME: Archie
can destroy dribbling
great dead·ball kicks...

WEAKNESSES: Can be selfish and not pass. Heading can definitely be improved. Loses confidence too easily.

It was a perfect sunlit morning as Dino FC trained beneath the vast shadow of Mount Rumble.

Gwen Corythosaurus glided past Cyril Stegosaurus as if he wasn't there, drew back her webbed left foot and hammered a shot past Pteradonna, the team's young goalie.

Steggy Stegoceras (the team's hard-headed and very grumpy defender) shook his head at the sight of Cyril, on all fours by the edge of the penalty area.

NO PACE!

Steggy rated himself way above everyone else in the squad and so never worried about transfer speculation. But their conversation was enough to worry Cyril, who looked across to the touch-line to where Terry was taking notes.

The boss had promised him he wouldn't be transferred but football was a tough game and things changed fast, Cyril knew that. What if Steggy was right?

Terry blew a whistle to bring the practice match to an end, and shouted to the squad that he wanted them to form a circle while he gave them some news.

Cyril's heart began pounding like the home supporters' match day drum.

THUD!
THUD!
THUD!

Terry thanked the team for a good training session and said it would stand them in good stead for the match on Saturday. And then he shuffled a little awkwardly. He looked at Cyril and then at the ground.

GULP!

JOSÉ... COULD I SEE YOU IN MY OFFICE FOR A CHAT, PLEASE?

"I wonder what they want to talk about?" asked Marcus Diplodocus, who had a small brain and never knew much about what was going on.

"Well I don't think they'll be discussing lunch," answered Steggy, sarcastically.

"Lunch!" announced Marcus.

Terry put down his shell-phone and told José to take a seat. José nodded and sat opposite his boss.

"I imagine you want to know why I've asked you in here?" Terry began, hoping José wouldn't be too upset at what he was about to say.

But José's face wore a big grin.

Terry tried not to raise his eyebrows too high. "Er, yes...that is to say...um, I decided to put you up for sale and another team is...indeed interested in buying you. I just took the call. We've agreed the fee and I've accepted their bid."

José jumped delightedly to his feet and punched the air in celebration.

"Who wants me?" jabbered the excited forward.

REAL HETERODONTOSAURUS? BAYERN BRACHIOPOD? AJAX ALLOSAURUS?

"Er, not quite," answered Terry. "It's, um...Ichthyosaur Thistle..."

"Who?" asked José, blankly. He'd never heard of them.

"Er, they play in Sedimentary Division Three. I think they're quite an ambitious team. Or was that *amphibious*? Either way I hope you'll be very happy there."

José now looked rather cross. This wasn't the sort of move he had in mind at all.

"Uh, it's too late, José. I'm sorry but let's face it, you were never happy here..." Terry consulted his player notes.

José looked outraged.

"I'm sorry," said Terry, "but the deal is done."

A disappointed José flounced out of the manager's office feeling very hard done by. He'd wanted a transfer but not to a tiny team like this.

Terry was about to head off when his chairman, Danny Deinonychus, suddenly loomed in front of him. Terry and Danny didn't always get on but Terry felt pleased at the day's progress.

"The deal has been done, Mr. Deinonychus," he announced, proudly. But something shifty in Danny's eyes made him worry. Had there been a last minute hitch?

"Sorry," began Danny, not looking Terry in the eye, "but I've just been speaking to the Ichthyosaur chairman…"

"What change is that?" asked Terry, with deep foreboding.

"In the end they decided they didn't want José," answered Danny, looking oddly cheerful now. "I pointed out he was very injury prone."

"Who?" asked Terry, fearing he was about to lose one of his star players.

There was a long pause before Danny finally answered.

Events moved quickly as they often do in the
world of dinosaur football. Terry was
manager of Dino FC, but it was Danny
Deinonychus who owned the team. Which
is why, in no time at all, Terry had said a
sad farewell to his squad, and found himself
standing outside the windswept entrance
to Ichthyosaur Thistle FC.

ICHTHYOSAUR
THISTLE FC

It was a small ground, set in the middle of a dark overgrown hollow, and seeing it made Terry's heart sink. He didn't know any of their players and he was already missing his old teammates. It took all his determination just to walk into the Ichthyosaur ground and introduce himself.

Thistle's manager, an elderly dinosaur called Giorgio Di Brontosaurus, was there to greet him.

Terry smiled shyly as Giorgio showed him around and told him that there would be a training session in ten minutes. He handed Terry a pale blue and white Thistle shirt with a number three on the back. How Terry wished it was a yellow Dino FC shirt!

Back in the shadows of Mount Rumble, Danny Deinonychus had assembled a shocked and saddened Dino FC team and was giving them the latest news. Not only had Terry left the club but they now had a new caretaker manager.

"Me," continued Danny, unaware of the stunned silence around him.

"I've watched quite a lot of football since I bought this dump and I think I've got the hang of it. It's only twelve dinosaurs kicking a ball around."

"Eleven," interrupted Celia.

"Eleven," nodded Danny.

"The goalie," glowered Pteradonna.

"I thought Terry was hopeless but this guy might be even worse…" whispered Steggy to Cyril Stegosaurus, standing alongside him.

Terry's first training session as a Thistle player had begun.

Ichthyosaur Thistle seemed to be a very tough-tackling team – especially when Terry had the ball. Every time he touched it, somebody clattered into him.

But what was even worse than the physical challenges was that no one spoke to Terry. Gone was the laughter and joking he was used to at Dino FC. Here there was just silence and the sound of Giorgio Di Brontosaurus bellowing out his instructions:

It wasn't the sort of football Terry liked and he wished with all his heart that he was back at Dino FC.

But things were no better at his old club. The first training session under Danny Deinonychus had just finished and no one was happy.

HE DOESN'T KNOW THE FIRST THING ABOUT FOOTBALL...

OR THE SECOND...

"Crumbs, if those two are agreeing, things must be bad," observed Steggy, having a cold shower in the dressing cave.

"We need to get Terry back," said Cyril with a note of desperation in his voice.

"But how?" asked José, nursing a flaking toenail.

Steggy shook his head gloomily. "The transfer deadline closes at midnight tomorrow."

IF WE DON'T GET HIM BACK BY THEN, WE'LL BE STUCK WITH THAT DOZY DEINONYCHUS FOR THE REST OF THE SEASON!

It was too terrible to contemplate!

It had begun to rain in the forest where
Terry's new club tree house was located.
Aching and bruised after his training session,
the weary triceratops was looking forward
to a good night's sleep. He missed his friends
and teammates, but tried to look on the
bright side despite the wind and the rain

lashing his new home. He was learning new skills (how to jump over tackles from your teammates), and new tactics (kicking the ball anywhere just to get rid of it).

I guess if I can play good football here then I can play it anywhere, he thought, as he got changed into his pyjamas and prepared to go to sleep.

Terry closed his eyes and felt the steady patter of rain on leaves, and the wind rustling angrily through the dark forest that surrounded him...

In Dinosaur Valley the next day dawned bright and clear with a vivid blue sky drawn over the hills and volcanoes.

Training wasn't for another four hours, but the Dino FC squad had already gathered together outside Cyril's home.

MORNING!

"The only way out of this mess is for the club to buy Terry back," announced Cyril once everyone had quietened down.

"Danny will never agree," said Steggy, shaking his bony head. "He's as mean as they come!"

"So we'll have to find the money ourselves," shouted out a determined Gwen Corythosaurus. She was a big fan of Terry as a manager – he'd helped her game a lot with his expert coaching style. "How about if we all donated a week's wages?"

There was a long silence.

José Heterodontosaurus looked at his injured nail. Steggy's eyebrows knitted together. Eric looked at Albert and Albert looked at Eric.

"I'll put my wages in," said Archie Opteryx just when it seemed none of the squad would ever speak again. Gwen nodded approvingly.

And soon pretty well everyone except Steggy had agreed to donate their wages to a new "transfer Terry back" fund.

Even Steggy offered half of his wages. "I've got a birthday coming up, so I do need to keep the rest back for a present."

"Whose birthday?" asked Celia Coelophysis.

MINE.

Of course the team had no way of knowing if all that week's wages would be enough to buy Terry back – they could only hope.

The next stage was to meet Danny Deinonychus and tell him of their plan.

"Who will be our spokesperson?" asked Cyril.

Steggy immediately volunteered, and then got very cross when Celia told him that might not be a good idea as he tended to get cross with people.

"Rubbish," Steggy snapped angrily and then went quiet when he realized he'd just proved her point. The squad decided that Celia herself would be the best choice to explain their plan to Danny, and they set off for the training ground hoping with all their hearts that their scheme would succeed. A whole season with Danny as their manager awaited them if it didn't!

Ichthyosaur Thistle were playing a reserve team match and Terry Triceratops was on the bench. Squeezed onto the end of it actually, as there wasn't much room with all the other muscular well-built subs his team had.

Thistle were three goals down and manager Giorgio was in a bad mood.

Terry took off his tracksuit and began to warm up. He needed to because it was another grey, wet day.

While Terry was doing some stretches, Ichthyosaur Thistle conceded a fourth goal and Giorgio kicked his drinks container onto the pitch in disgust.

As he prepared to run onto the pitch he looked across for a moment and saw Giorgio talking on his shell-phone. The elderly brontosaurus suddenly gestured to Terry to sit down again.

Terry felt disappointed, he'd really wanted to get onto the pitch and try and prove his worth. Giorgio came over to him.

I AM SORRY, TERENCE, BUT THERE HAS BEEN A DEVELOPMENT...

"A development?" asked Terry, looking puzzled. "Yes, it seems you are no longer a Thistle player!" Terry wandered down the players' tunnel in a daze. Had he been transferred again? It didn't make sense...

And if he had been transferred, where to? And then he glimpsed a familiar figure, a figure that gave him a clue.

BOSS!

It was Cyril Stegosaurus.

And suddenly, from behind him appeared the rest of the squad.

"I-I don't understand," stammered Terry.

"We persuaded Danny to sign you back again," explained Celia.

A huge smile crossed Terry's face. His tail wagged. He felt really happy for the first time in ages. But then another question...

HOLD ON, WHY WOULD DANNY RE-SIGN ME? WOULDN'T THAT HAVE COST HIM MONEY?!

Terry's teammates fell silent, too modest and embarrassed to explain what they'd done.

"They gave their own wages to get you back," came a voice from behind Terry.

It was Giorgio Di Brontosaurus. "You must have great team spirit in your club," he continued.

MY PLAYERS WOULD NOT GIVE A HALF-EATEN BUSH TO KEEP ME IN MY JOB!

Terry looked at the team and nodded.

YOU'RE RIGHT, GIORGIO, WE DO HAVE GREAT SPIRIT BECAUSE... THIS LOT ARE THE BEST!

In his very smart executive tree house, chairman Danny was counting the club funds with a big smile along his tooth-lined jaw. He'd somehow managed to sell one of his own players and then get him back for free.

I *love football*, he thought, counting the cash for a second time just for the fun of it and wondering what to spend the money on. *I could do with a new watch... And maybe a nice holiday.*

It was hot and it was humid. But still Terry made the team play another session of "head" tennis.

Gwen Corythosaurus turned to Archie Opteryx. "Makes you wonder if we did the right thing getting him back!"

As Terry watched there was still one player who didn't seem to be making much effort – José Heterodontosaurus.

Terry could take it no more. Whilst the others kept playing, the Dino FC boss took his big striker to one side and gave him a stern look.

"Okay, José... I don't know what your problem is this morning and I don't really care. I just want to tell you something..."

José wiped his brow feebly.

IF YOU COULD BE QUICK, POR FAVOR...I FEELING A LITTLE...FAINT...

"You're very lucky to be at this club," Terry began, with real passion in his voice. "I know because I've been at another club and let me tell you it's not a bed of floral ferns out there."

José nodded uneasily, as Terry's words got through. Maybe he could try a little harder. If it had been him who had been transferred to Ichthyosaur Thistle, how would he have fared? Not very well from what Terry told him.

"The transfer deadline is closed now," continued the Dino FC boss. "So you're still part of my squad, José. Let's see if we can make this work?"

José nodded.

Terry told José he'd see him tomorrow for a game against Troodon Wanderers, and hoped his little pep talk had done some good.

The day had dawned cloudy and overcast. Dino FC were hoping to move into the top half of the Dino Premier League table with

a win against their newly-promoted opponents. Troodon Wanderers were a big club who'd fallen on hard times and almost become extinct, but now they were on their way back and Terry was expecting a tough game.

Dino FC's manager had decided to start the game with an experienced old head up front – Ollie Oviraptor.

As well as an old head, Ollie also had old legs, so Terry suspected he might not be able to last the full ninety minutes. If he didn't then he would bring on José and see if his striker had responded to the talk they'd had the day before.

José looked a little grumpy when he learned he wouldn't be starting the game.

Dino FC started well. Archie's trickery bought space for Celia and her snap shot almost broke the net.

Next, Ollie Oviraptor turned back the years when he dropped his shoulder, ignored his creaking knees and jinked past two defenders and rifled home for a second goal.

Terry and his team celebrated but the game wasn't in the bag yet. Wanderers pulled a goal back from a corner and Dino FC's manager spotted that Ollie was struggling with an injury.

Terry waved to the touch-line and signalled José to replace his veteran centre forward.

As José prepared to come onto the field, Troodon Wanderers equalized.

Then, Eric Allosaurus brought down their number eight with a scything challenge and earned himself a red rock.

Albert started arguing with his brother about what a foolish challenge he'd made and got sent off as well!

Dino FC were down to nine players. As José trotted onto the pitch, Terry told his centre forward the team needed him to play his very best if they were going to hold on. José nodded.

Ten per cent more like, thought Terry. But during the remaining twenty minutes José did his best to prove Terry wrong.

He ran like a demon. He covered more ground than a herd of brachiosauruses. He made last-ditch tackles, he urged on his teammates, and with five minutes left he got the ball around the halfway line and raced towards the opposition goal.

Three-two to Dino FC! A delighted Terry turned to Cyril as the crowd went wild.

"What message is that?" asked Cyril.

"That this is a great club to play for and that he is lucky to be here."

Cyril nodded.

As the game ended, José lingered on the pitch signing autographs for Dino FC fans.

Terry sought out his wayward star and gave him a congratulatory slap on the back.

José nodded in agreement. As Terry and the rest of the team vanished down the tunnel, José took out his shell-phone and called his agent.

"Yes… I score a brilliant goal…and everyone says I am the dinosaur of the match… Si…so I think next season…I will stay with this team. No…I am not ill…I have a little injury but no, I am okay…I think I like it here. At Dino FC. Yes… I am contento."

Eddie

On the other end of the line Eddie fell silent. In all his time working with José he had never heard him sound so happy and relaxed!

Young fans

Terry and Cyril were walking home, still tired after their efforts playing with nine men.

But Terry was in high spirits.

"No...I'm just a beginner. But what I did learn is that Dino FC is a great little club and I'm determined to take us all the way to the top."

"You'll do it, boss."

And as the moon slowly began to rise,
Terry and Cyril continued their walk home
dreaming of future glory for their team...

MEET THE PLAYERS IN DINO FC
– THE CRAZIEST TEAM IN THE JURASSIC WORLD!

RUMBLEY STADIUM – THE DINO FC GROUND

PTERADONNA 1

POSITION: goalkeeper
SKILLS: flying
LIKES: catching crosses
DISLIKES: non-football days
FOOTY FACT: the youngest member of the squad

STEGGY STEGOCERAS 2

POSITION: defender
SKILLS: good at marking opponents
LIKES: grumbling
DISLIKES: being told what to do
FOOTY FACT: applied for the manager's job but Terry got it

MARCUS DIPLODOCUS 3

POSITION: defender
SKILLS: great in the air
LIKES: heading the ball
DISLIKES: quick forwards
FOOTY FACT: last season won 76% of all headers

TERRY TRICERATOPS 4

POSITION: manager and fullback
SKILLS: tactician
LIKES: tough talking
DISLIKES: defensive football
FOOTY FACT: only player-manager in the DPL

CYRIL STEGOSAURUS — 5

POSITION: **fullback**

SKILLS: **following instructions**

LIKES: **moving slowly**

DISLIKES: **anyone criticizing Terry, "the boss"**

FOOTY FACT: **the vice-captain**

ALBERT ALLOSAURUS — 6

POSITION: **midfield**

SKILLS: **dealing with tricky forwards**

LIKES: **arguing with his twin**

DISLIKES: **Eric. Refs**

FOOTY FACT: **once got 21 red cards in a season**

GWEN CORYTHOSAURUS — 7

POSITION: **midfield**

SKILLS: **controlling midfield**

LIKES: **playing in the rain**

DISLIKES: **hot temperatures**

FOOTY FACT: **the team's free kick specialist**

ARCHIE OPTERYX — 8

POSITION: **winger**

SKILLS: **great dribbler**

LIKES: **doing ball tricks**

DISLIKES: **bumpy pitches**

FOOTY FACT: **takes the team's corners**

ERIC ALLOSAURUS

9

POSITION: midfield

SKILLS: tackling, marking

LIKES: arguing with his twin

DISLIKES: Albert. Refs

FOOTY FACT: once got 20 red cards in a season

CELIA COELOPHYSIS

10

POSITION: forward

SKILLS: fast and graceful

LIKES: looking good on the pitch

DISLIKES: tackling or being tackled

FOOTY FACT: fastest player on the team

JOSÉ HETERODONTOSAURUS

11

POSITION: forward

SKILLS: falling over in the box

LIKES: winning penalties

DISLIKES: most things

FOOTY FACT: on average only fit for 2.3 games per season

OLLIE OVIRAPTOR

12

POSITION: utility player

SKILLS: football brain, experience

LIKES: resting after the match

DISLIKES: playing 90 minutes

FOOTY FACT: has been a pro for 22 seasons

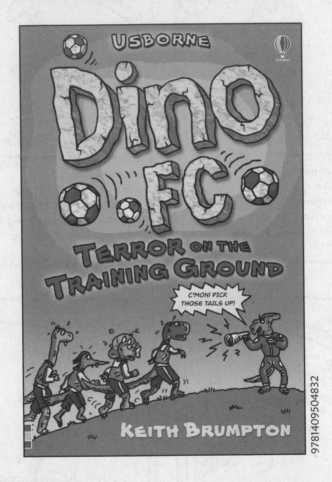

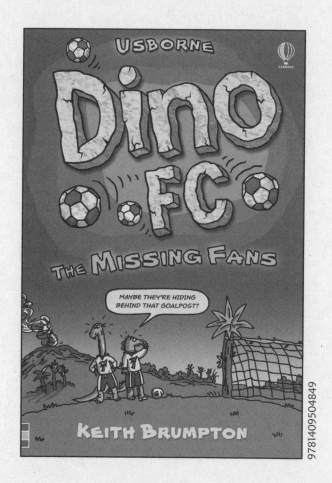

Dino FC's fans have deserted them, but Terry's got
great plans to attract new supporters...if only
the players could remember his instructions!

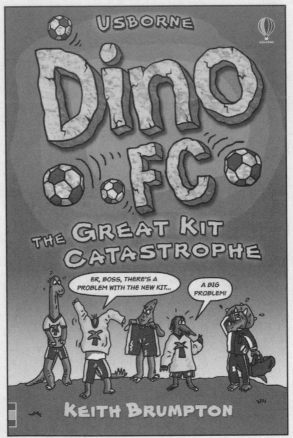

Dino FC's old kit is falling apart at the seams.
But the new kit is a catastrophe. Are the team's
chances of victory in tatters again?

Could rival team manager, Alex McTeeth,
have anything to do with the mysterious
disappearance of Dino FC's flying goalie?

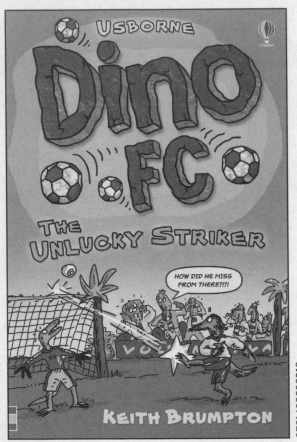

Dino FC's star striker, Archie Opteryx, is having a run of bad luck. Can he return to form - or is it all over for this rising dino star?

For more action-packed reads head to